THE

LURKING

HAYDEN GRIBBLE

ISBN 978-1-9998659-5-5

Printed and bound by Lightning Source, Milton Keynes.

www.facebook.com/haydengribleauthor

www.haydengribble.net

For you

Also by the author

The CAPTAIN RANDOM Adventures

Captain Random vs the Sandman
Captain Random and the Eater of Souls

Other titles by the author

The Man In The Corner
Tales From Another Me
Child Out Of Time: Growing Up With Doctor Who In
The Wilderness Years

I

The car negotiated the wet road as the rain continued to pelt it with anger. Inside the small hatchback, Rob was trying desperately to ensure he would make it home on time. For all the nights to be kept late at work, it had to be this one. The one evening he had been preparing for ever since he had started planning the marriage proposal.

He knew he hadn't been the easiest of boyfriends. There were more idiosyncrasies in his flawed persona than there were menu choices at an all you can eat Chinese buffet. Sure, he spent too much time gaming, or going out with friends, but at least his heart was in the right place.

At least, that's what he hoped she thought. He didn't really know.

Rob never understood the need to open up about his feelings to her.

Yet now, with the ring nestled safely in the small box the shop had provided him, rocking backwards and forwards in the cup holder of his black Fiat Punto.

Rob thought better of its unsafe housing and popped the box in his jacket pocket. It would be typical of him to somehow mislay it, even though it was in plain sight.

He could lose a chair in an empty room. Sorting through his memories, stored in the cluttered drawers of his mind, he winced at the high probability that he had done just that at some point in his life.

His thoughts returned to his plans for the evening. He was about to open up in ways in which he had never done before.

Claire knew that she was loved. She just wanted him around more.

She'd complained that she hadn't anticipated a life of nights in by herself on a frequent basis when she had asked Rob to move in with her.

In fact, she'd dreamt of the opposite.

Warm, cosy evenings cuddled up on the sofa, a dinner for two in the oven whilst they channel hopped their way through the night.

She thought that co-habiting would bring them closer together but he just seemed so distant. Like a man at sea, he just seemed to let life wash around him and take him wherever the tide dictated.

He was drifting, and he knew it.

Rob turned the headlamps to full beam. His journey home was going to take a little longer than he had hoped.

To compound the misery of having to stay at work late to make up for the time he had dithered and dallied on the right ring during his lunch break, an accident had taken place on his usual route and he was now going down the dark country back roads. The sat-nav on his phone was draining the battery but he trusted it implicitly. As long as it got him home before seven, he was going to be okay.

As the car swung around another sharp corner on the one lane road, the cabin illuminated. Rob looked down at the phone and noticed it was ringing. It was Claire.

Maintaining his focus on the road, he swiped for the accept sign.

'Babe! Hi!'

'Where the hell are you?'

Claire seemed stern. Rob hated it when she sounded like that.

'Just making my way home. What's up?'

'What now? You're so late!'

'No, I'm not. Sat navs taken me another way. There's been an accident on the A1307. It's taking me through some back roads but I should still be back by 7.'

Claire sighed. 'You haven't reset your clock on your phone, have you?'

Rob's face dropped. He squinted in the blackness at the clock on the dashboard.

6.21.

'Shit.'

'Yep.'

'So, it's...'

'Twenty past seven, yeah.'

'Claire, I'm sorry-'

'You promised me.'

'I know, babe, I'm sorry. Look, we can catch the later showing. I'm making good time. I'll be home before you know it.'

There was an awkward silence.

'Rob…it's been six months. I can count the date nights we've had on one hand in that time.'

'I've got a good excuse this time; I'll tell you when I get home.'

'This time?' Claire scoffed. 'So you're saying that last week's excuse of forgetting to book the table because you'd lost the number was actually down to the fact that you'd completely forgotten what day it was?'

'Well…'

'It was my birthday, you arsehole!'

'Claire, please-'

'You know, I thought us moving in together would bring us closer, but it hasn't, has it? It's just an excuse for having a place for you and your mates to chill, leaving me to clean up all the mess. I'm just here to accommodate your stupid lifestyle and save you money on your bills.'

'Oh come on, now you're just being out of order!' Rob raged.

He didn't like hearing what a useless boyfriend he was, even if he knew it was the truth.

'You know what? When my friends say that they struggle to see what I see in you, it hurts, especially knowing that you couldn't give a toss what I want.'

'Will you just shut up a minute, Claire? Of course I care, that's not fair!'

'Fair?' Claire screamed, her tones quacking with emotion. 'I'll tell you what's fair. Fair is keeping your promises. Fair is being there for the one you love. Fair is putting other people before you sometimes. You don't know the meaning of the word.'

Rob gripped the steering wheel so tightly his knuckles began to turn white.

'You have no idea, Claire, you have no idea.'

'Don't make this about your job again, you prick.'

'I'm not, if you'd just give me a chance to-'

'No!' she cried. 'I am fed up of giving you chances. I hope you took your key with you cos there won't be anyone here to let you in tonight!'

And with that, the call went dead.

'Claire!'

She had hung up.

Rob tried desperately to call her back. He had to make it better. He couldn't lose her.

Not tonight of all nights. He took his eyes off the road, fingering the screen furiously. His mind was full of fury and confusion. His night couldn't get any worse.

And then it did.

The car's front tyres slipped and Rob completely lost control of the vehicle. He grappled in vain with the steering wheel but it was no use. The sound of screeching rubber on tarmac shot through his ears.

Rob closed his eyes as he braced for the inevitable. He was going to crash.

In a matter of seconds, the vehicle swung wildly off the road and hit a small tree stump. Rob screamed as the car flew in the air before smashing down on its side into the soft, boggy earth in a dark, lonely field. It rolled a couple of times before coming to a halt, nothing more now than a ball of twisted metal.

The Fiat groaned as it dug a furrow in the dirt. The pitter patter of falling rain drops was the only sound that filled the air now. Inside the wreck, Rob lay in his seat, silent, still, dead to the world.

Droplets started to seep through the broken driver's window and proceeded to drip on his unconscious face. Slowly, he came around.

He opened his eyes and blinked back from the sweet embrace of sleep into his waking nightmare. He shrieked, startled and distressed.

'Oh my god, oh my god, shit!' he gasped.

His limbs flailed in panic as he was bolted fast to his seat. Yet he was alive, no harm done.

How? He'd look for answers to that question later. He had to get out.

'Help! Someone!'

Nothing.

Rob made for the seatbelt release.

It was jammed. He pulled on it in desperation, grappling until his hands wore against the fabric of the harness and managed to wriggle himself free. A lifelong sufferer of claustrophobia, his eyes were wide with panic. He started to cry, kicking the windscreen with all his might to escape his prison.

After several meaningful jabs with his feet, the windscreen, which was already crumpled by the devastation of the accident, began to pop out of its position. He could smell freedom.

And something else.

Sniffing harder, there was a pungent smell that was beginning to fill the air. It was getting stronger.

Suddenly, Rob realised what it was.

It was petrol.

'Holy fuck!' he cried. Kicking like mad, Rob finally managed to puncture a hole big enough to climb through.

Picking up his mobile phone, which had fallen onto the passenger seat, he placed his hands on the windscreen rim, ignoring the small shards of glass that were now sinking into his palms and pulled himself out of the wreckage.

The thick mud gripped itself around his ankles and tried to hold him down like hands hauling him to the ground.

He slipped and stuck to the bog and tried with all his might to get as far away from the accident as quickly as he could. He'd seen the films.

A massive explosion was imminent and he was right in the way of the impending fireball.

Rob shook with fear as he continued his getaway. The rain continued to lash down on his cold, shocked person. A short time passed and he allowed himself a quick glance over his shoulder.

There were no Hollywood explosions, no deadly jets of fire shooting high into the air, no twisted shards of metal showering down. There wasn't even a tiny flame. The movies had lied to him.

He sighed, catching his breath. How could this happen? On tonight of all nights. The night he had promised to himself that he was going to change for the better, for Claire, and fate had conspired to ruin it. He held out his hand and glanced at his phone, squinting through the heavy rain drops streaming down his face.

No bars.

Rob pulled his shirt collar up around his neck and looked around him. There was no one else on the road. He must have been the only car for a few miles. What was he to do? Wait in the freezing rain in the vain hope someone would happen to drive by? Or should he walk?

Both were not the most attractive of propositions.

He had to find shelter, somewhere to collect his thoughts, get out of the torrential downpour and, hopefully, get some signal to call for help and apologise to Claire.

The young man searched through the gloomy wet night. There were no street lights, nothing. Except…

He squinted. Yes, there was something in the far distance, across the field, past the road and trench that had caused Rob's crash, on the other side of the void.

It looked like a control tower.

Rob walked towards it to get a closer look.

He stopped for a second and fumbled in his jacket pocket.

The ring was still in there. He transferred it to his inside breast pocket, hoisted the sopping wet jacket over his head and made for the tower.

As he moved closer and closer, he could make out more of the mysterious tower's structure.

There seemed to be a large hangar situated at the base of it. Oddly, he had driven down this road countless times. It was a straight, lonely stretch and as far as he knew it, not many cars made the same journey, favouring the main road.

How had he never seen it before?

Then again, he thought to himself, it had taken him three months to notice Claire's advances towards him at university. It had taken him even longer to realise she was utterly besotted with him. He wasn't the most observant of men.

Pity. If she hadn't have gotten to know him, with his lackadaisical approach to life and all things in his world, where his ability to emote his true affections was stunted worse than a flower without sun and water, maybe she'd be living a happier life than she was right now.

Rob shook his head clear of these negative thoughts the best he could. He decided to pick up the pace, despite the ache in his legs, no doubt already bruising from the impact of the crash. His breathe was visible in the cold storm, little clouds of exhaustion emitting from his heaving lungs.

Thankfully, he managed to get to what he surmised was the front door. He tried the handle.

Locked.

Of course it was.

He blinked up into the rainy sky and looked for another entrance. Even in the gloom he could tell that the tower was in a state of severe decay.

Rob slipped in the bog as he trod around the tower. No side door falling off its hinges.

Nothing.

The light of hope in Rob's heart was beginning to fade. Unless he could get in, he would have to face walking back onto the main road. Even then, who would stop for a sopping wet man like him?

He decided the hangar may afford him better luck. Chancing himself, he came across a nook slightly ajar on the main hangar doors and he thanked this crumb of fortune. This was more like it, he thought. The metal was coarse with rust as his fingers tried desperately to find a door handle or something to help him prise his way towards sanctuary. He took a look up at the abandoned wreck. It looked huge, cloaked by the darkness of the night until Rob pretty much fell onto one of its outer walls. It also looked less impregnable than the tower.

Using the torch on his phone, he searched the hangar doors.

There was a chain binding the main handles together but still enough of a gap for him to squeeze through to shelter.

He maneuvered his dripping hands over the phone screen, fumbling to turn the torch off and trying even harder not to drop it in the boggy mud. As he pocketed the phone, he glanced at the battery life on the top of the screen. 36 percent. It should be enough.

No bars of signal still, though. Rob put the phone away and sucked his tubby belly in.

Crouching down, he wriggled underneath the chain, the skin on his back rubbing against his clothes as his body pinched between the gap.

He winced as the rusty metal threatened to pincer him to death. Rob took another deep breath, small tears of pain forming in the corners of his eyes.

Inch by inch, he pushed himself inside.

As he felt his flesh tear under the strain, he yelped and with one final push, fell flat with his torso finally free of the vice, finally out of the rain.

He took a moment to regain his breath before kicking his legs into the dry confines of the hangar.

Rob scrunched his shoulders up as he lay on the dirty floor, feeling his injuries.

Although his clothes were wet through, he could feel the impact of the crash on his body where his flesh had been cut.

Large areas of his back and stomach that were red with pain.

Bruises and slashes were evident and were hard to ignore.

He hissed through his teeth as he poked his wounds with his trembling fingers.

Picking himself up, he felt the dusty floor. Steadily rising to his full height, he clicked his back and peered into the darkness, holding his phone out in front acting as a torch.

Whatever this place was, it had been abandoned for years. As the distant shower of rain pinged quietly on the high roof, Rob was reminded of his predicament.

His car was a write-off, his relationship in tatters and still there was no signal on his phone, the battery decreasing with every passing minute.

Taking in his surroundings, he wondered if there may be an old landline telephone hanging around the derelict building.

Then he could call Claire and tell her he was sorry for everything.

Surely she would forgive him given the kind of night he was having.

Surely.

The hangar was cold and unwelcoming. He would need to find something warm to help stop him shivering.

Breathing into his hands to keep them warm, he decided to take a look around.

From high within the hangar, the creature stirred.

It had been a long time since it had company. Its nostrils flared, pricked by the sense of tantalising fresh meat, picking up the scent of the stranger taking shelter in its prison.

The creature gurgled softly to itself and unfurled its powerful frame for the first time in decades.

The smell of blood had awoken it from its slumber...

The hangar was dank and dark, the stench of rust and damp swamped Rob as he continued to look around.

Suddenly, a clang of metal somewhere in the hangar made him jump out of his skin, emitting a short shriek of terror in the process. He clutched his chest and steadied his breathing. The shock soon ebbed away until there was nothing more than the soothing sound of rain coming down onto the roof.

His mind began to race. The dark, mysterious hangar was making him think things, imagine terrible visions of doom, but then a more rational voice started to whisper in his mind.

This place is ancient, deserted. Man up, nothing's going to hurt you. Just find some signal, call Claire and get the hell home, stick to your plan and everything will be okay.

He sighed. It must have been a rope or something snapping somewhere near him, causing some airplane part to fall over. Maybe he even accidentally broke something.

Shaking his head, he walked on.

He needed to find a light switch quick otherwise it would run out of juice even sooner.

Edging his way along the wall, he felt for the light switch and breathed a sigh of relief as his wet fingers finally found one. He clicked it on. Nothing. He tried again. Still nothing.

'Oh, come on!' he cried.

No matter how many times he turned the switch on and off, it made no difference to the lighting within the deserted hangar. After a time, he stopped. He gazed down hopefully at his phone. Still no signal bars. His battery was also running down fast.

'Fuck!' he exclaimed, pocketing it. He would have to conserve its energy, but how did he do it?

He knew there was a setting somewhere but without googling it, he wouldn't have a clue. If he had signal, he'd be able to look up what this place was and it might explain why he had never seen it before.

Then again, he was alone, all by himself in a mysterious place.

Why couldn't he just take a look around, whilst he waited for the storm to ease off, and find out that way?

It wasn't like there would be anyone around to stop him. Why couldn't he quell his curiosity? Who knew, maybe he would find a torch along the way! Rob furrowed his brow and ploughed on.

It lurks...

The darkness embraced Rob's cautious outline as he rounded into a corridor that looked like it fed to another part of the hangar.

He squinted and could make out light fittings, ancient and damaged, dangling limply from the ceiling like lifeless bodies from a hangman's noose.

He held his arms out, feeling his way down the narrow passageway, stumbling as he walked over rubbish which had been undisturbed for years.

'This place must have been abandoned a long time ago,' he said out loud.

'Oh great, now I'm talking to myself. I'm starting to lose it.'

Another sudden clatter of metal caused Rob to shriek again. He starred wildly into the blackness.

'It's just your imagination Robert, it's just your imagination.'

He continued down the corridor and admitted to himself that maybe speaking out loud wouldn't be such a bad thing.

It would do his nerves the world of good for a start.

But what if there was someone or something in here with him?

'It'll only be a homeless bloke, don't you worry about that. Hey, maybe that's who's making all that noise!'

Rob turned on his heels and began to make his way back into the main hangar.

'Hey! It's alright, I won't hurt you. I'm lost, can you help me? Hello?'

It heard him.

His shrill tones echoed in the main chamber. He could only be less than twenty metres away. The stalker growled softly to itself and continued its slow amble towards its prey...

'Hello?' Rob hollered again. Nothing.

He tutted to himself and decided to continue down the corridor to see where it led him.

Before long he came to some double doors, which lay splintered with broken glass scattered across the dusty floor.

Rob trod carefully, doing his best not to pick up any fragments in the holes in his shoes. His socks were already sodden from the rain and muddied by the trek across the field, the last thing he wanted was a piece of glass lodging itself in the sole of his foot.

Claire was always telling him to chuck his trainers out. But they were his favourite pair and expensive to replace. What about the sentimental value of them?

How could she ever understand the satisfaction they brought him when he wore them during his five-a-side's semi-final victory over Simon Wallace's side? I mean, sure, they had lost the final, but to get one over Simon, after the humiliation he had made Rob feel so often throughout their years at school? To see the look on his face as Rob slotted the winning penalty past him.

He had relented to wearing them when she was not with him and right now, Claire was far out of the picture.

Plus, there was no way he wanted Claire to be right.

Suddenly, Rob cried out in pain. He clutched his right leg close to him and fell through what remained of the double doors, hitting the deck on the other side, on more tiny shards of what used to be the windows.

He crawled to the side, the pain still burning hot. He whimpered as he felt along his sole. There it was. A sheet of glass was sticking out of his foot at a bad angle. He swore, loudly, and pulled it out of the hole in his shoe.

The shard was roughly two inches long and at least a quarter of the length had embedded itself within the ball of his foot.

He felt the wound and winced.

A dull throb began to pulsate around the affected area.

'Shit!' he swore again.

The sound he had heard before ringed from behind him, ceasing his pitiful cries of agony and frustration.

That same sound. What did it sound like? The sound of metal yawning open, scraping across itself. What was it?

'Look, stop it, whoever you are! Game over. I'm not playing. If you're trying to scare me then it's not working, so piss off!'

The scraping continued. That hadn't happened before.

Rob began to panic. He was scared. Terrified. And he'd ruined his favourite trainers.

II

Rob shimmied his way up the wall and tried to put some weight on his injured foot.

He winced a little as he placed his sole flat on the surface.

He couldn't do it, he'd have to hop and hope whoever was tormenting him got tired and left him alone. There was no way he was going to go and find them.

They probably didn't mean him any harm whether it be psychological or physical.

Rob wasn't one to have an over-stimulated imagination but he damned well was creating all sorts of terrifying scenarios in his head right now.

He was no action hero but he was going to try and outrun them. Whoever - or whatever – they were.

'Come on, brain, this is no time to panic,' he muttered.

He squeezed his eyes and began to limp in the opposite direction.

'Come on, Rob, be more Bruce Willis. Be more Bruce Willis.'

It picked up another scent, one that was growing stronger and stronger. Its nostril flared. Iron and red platelets. Its eyes grew wider and burnt like two terrible pits of death.

Blood.

It lurked...

Rob found his way into another part of the hangar entirely.

Now his surroundings resembled more of a more conventional place of work.

In fact, he could swear that in the terrible darkness, although his eyes had adjusted well to the lack of light in the building, there were what looked like offices. Deciding to get out of sight, he tried the door to one of them.

It was locked. Of course it was locked.

He checked the name tag that stuck out just above his eye level.

Prof Whittaker. PhD Biology.

'Biology? What's a biologist doing in a place like this?'

He stepped back and tried another of the doors, one that was missing a name tag completely.

'Aha!' he cried quietly as finally, his luck was changing. The door knob was loose but unlocked.

Another scraping sound made him jump. It sounded closer this time.

Struggling to keep his composure, Rob scrambled at the knob and breathed a sigh of relief as it swung open, allowing him inside.

In the same swift movement, he shut the door quickly behind him and slid to the floor, an icy fear seeping out of every pore in his body.

It kept coming, dragging its tongue along the ground, following the path laid out by the tiny droplets of crimson, a trail that led to the creature's meal. It licked its lips in anticipation, the taste of food was overpowering, revitalized by the hunger it had stirred deep within its soul.

It lapped up the blood.

It made it thirstier, hungrier, than it had been in many, many years.

It lurked...

Rob's breathing was heavy with terror.

Now he was still, trying to make no sound, maybe he could hear it. There was something coming after him.

It wasn't his imagination after all.

He could hear it slobbering and imagined a horrific salivating mouth slobbering over the thought of tearing him to shreds.

He pictured in his mind a lion or a tiger perhaps? Could it be some escaped animal from a local zoo?

He was sure there was one close by. Didn't he take Claire there once? Yes, that must be it, he thought.

The creature growled softly. Rob did all he could to calm himself but it was next to impossible. Even if his breathing was becoming less audible, he swore he could hear his heart beating against his ribcage.

He wiped a trickle of sweat off his temple.

The sound of the thing that had been stalking him since he had broken into the abandoned hangar seemed so close, he swore he could feel its breath on the back of his neck.

The creature had come to a halt outside the office door. It whimpered gently to itself and rubbed its body against it. Rob closed his eyes and hugged his shoulders.

The whimper grew stronger and stronger, like the creature was revving up its engine.

Rob forced his sleeve into his mouth to stifle any scream.

The creature released a guttural, unearthly roar, so loud that the ground shook with its thunderous rage. Rob shrieked and crawled away from the door, scrambling for an exit from this hellish nightmare.

There wasn't one.

No door to make for, no window out of the hangar. His only way out was blocked.

The screeching demon began to hurl its frame against the door.

With its first effort, the hinge busted apart at the top.

Rob turned white.

He looked around him for cover, but with only a couple of stools, a table and a draw down blackboard in the room, his options for hiding places were limited.

The creature hurled itself again and this time nearly broke the whole door in two.

Rob dived out of the way, just as the beast tried a third time and burst through what was nothing more than splinter and glass into the office.

Rob managed to wedge himself behind the blackboard and desk and from the shadows glanced in terror from his hiding place.

It was no lion.

This was a creature from the depths of hell itself.

He could only make out the outline, but the creature, consumed by the gloomy darkness of the room, was too hard to make out.

It was as though the monster was at one with the dark.

The creature roared again.

Its screech sounded like nails down a chalkboard, slowed down and amplified. It surveyed the room, looking for the trail that had led it here.

The scent was overpowering, focusing its senses solely on what lie in wait.

It thrashed around the room, rearing up in front of the blackboard, it charged head first towards it. Rob hurled himself out of his hiding place and crashed into the debris as the monster crashed into the wall, crying out in pain as it fell to the ground. It writhed in agony, kicking and screaming as it held its head like a child would.

Rob made good of his opportunity and threw himself back onto his feet and with great effort hurdled over the decimated debris and out of the room.

He ran as fast as he could to get away from the monster, whose screech rang after him down the long, dark corridor. His ears still ringing, his foot throbbing and his head pounding like mad, he willed himself to keep going until he could hear the beast's cries no more.

Eventually at a safe distance, he finally collapsed onto his haunches, gulping hard at the air as he tried to get his breathe back.

Rob made for his pocket. His phone was still safely stored away. Delving deep, his hand was shaking as he pulled it close to him. Still no signal, no one to call for help. And worse still, the battery in the red. He squinted at the screen, his vision blurred by his panic. The phone only had 14 percent left.

He had to get out.

But how?

The monster was hot on his scent and blocking his way back to the main hangar.

'Oh god, come on. If you're really up there give me a break!' Rob pleaded.

He glanced back down the corridor. It had gone quiet. Maybe the creature was wounded and had gone off to lick its wounds?

No, he thought. It was still far too risky to go back.

No, he had to keep going and find a way out of this nightmare.

He took a deep breath and continued his journey onwards.

Black.

Nothingness.

It couldn't see a thing.

The creature began to stir, groaning like a wounded dog.

It blinked its eyes open and quickly fastened them shut. The pain was too much.

It would have to rest for a while, sleep, perhaps.

But not for long.

It would have its fun soon enough.

Hesitantly, Rob made his way into another room. It was as dark and bleak as the rest of the place.

There was also a stench so foul Rob put his damp sleeve over his face. It smelt like rotting food. He retched as he entered what looked like a small office.

He looked around him cautiously and closed the door, tempted to move a nearby filing cabinet into place to slow down the monster.

Whilst starting to lift the heavy object, he remembered the light work the creature had made of the door and realized it was futile.

The cabinet had fallen onto its side. Within moments, he wished he hadn't touched it.

He wasn't alone.

Rob recoiled in horror as he noticed a hand flopped over the cabinet. Even in the poor lighting, he knew what he was facing.

Every impulse in his body told him to run away and move on and yet he stayed, a morbid curiosity overwhelming him.

He knelt down next to the corpse and used a piece of rubble close to his feet to poke it onto its back.

Rob gazed into vacant, dead eyes that stared back at him. He proceeded to retch and vomit. Wiping his mouth with his arm, he couldn't take his eyes off it.

It was the body of a man and he had been there for a long, long time.

Strips of putrefied flesh dangled off his skeletal frame. His hair looked auburn but there was no other colour to be seen apart from grey. Rob looked around for something to cover the body with and settled for a long coat. He draped it over the corpse and backed away, knocking into a table in the process. He put his hands down to break his fall and fell onto what looked like a notepad.

Rob swiped it up and decided to take it with him. He didn't much fancy being in there any longer. Making his way deeper into the building, he eventually found what looked to him like a waiting room. Thanks to its high windows, a couple of feet above Rob's reach there appeared to be more visibility than in other parts of his prison.

Taking another cautious look around, he sat down in a nearby chair and began to study the pad.

The handwriting was neat, written in fine pencil but he was unable to read it. He had to get out and yet he was drawn to whatever secrets may have been scribbled down within. Maybe he would get an explanation as to what the hell that monster was that had been following him.

Rob sighed. He got his phone out again and used its glow to illuminate the paper.

Peering closer, he began to read.

TEST FOUR – CARRIED OUT BY DOCTOR WILLIAMS 08:00hrs 27th March 1943.

'1943!?' Rob gasped. Had this hangar really been abandoned that long?

He continued:

Report:

Tests confirm that the creature has the ability to adapt to its present surroundings. No sign of light deprivation or the need for dark vision enablers at it is able to see in both blinding light and darkness. No news yet on its armoured capability – test capacity for cellular rejuvenation in a day's time.

The creature is not yet deemed safe enough to warrant being relinquished of its shackles.

We continue to manipulate it using electrical impulses that seem to bend it to our will.

The writing ended. Rob flicked onto the next page.

TEST FIVE – CONDUCTED BY PROF BARCLAY AT 03:24hrs 28th March 1943.

The next test was brought forward by twelve hours at the behest of the Batallion General. Why, I was not aware until we were called to a briefing not long after breakfast.

It was of the highest urgency and many of us speculated on what the General had in mind next for our unearthly friend.

He had received orders from Whitehall which stipulated that now the Americans have been seen helping out with the war effort, the Prime Minister has suddenly got cold feet with the whole project.

This came as a shock to many of us present at the briefing and I started to worry about how we could dispose of such a creature.

I explained to the General that it was not likely that the subject could be put down in the conventional way of a lethal injection or death by firing squad.

He insisted he was not here to shut down the project, only to accelerate it, to show the cabinet that we truly had a weapon that would defeat Herr Hitler, his evil army and liberate Europe.

This might have sounded to the congregation like a fantastic idea at the time.

I must admit that although the creature is part my invention - in fact, may be my GREATEST triumph apart from my family - I am starting to grow concerned.

Our methods in establishing the creature's skills and capabilities seem to have caused much distress to our subject. With every electrical impulse we have created, it seemed to have swelled in size.

Biometrics have indicated that my suspicions are correct. Although the shocks have increased capacity and armoury of the skin, scans of the creature's brain patterns have also shown that we are damaging its neurological make-up.

In conclusion, conditioning the creature is making it less rational and less likely to carry out instructions we give it.

Rob gulped. Hard.

How had anyone not heard of this?

He checked his surroundings and flicked through the rest of the pad. Rob made out another entry in the pad.

PERSONAL – 14th April 1943.

The creature's become rather prone to violent episodes, with devastating results. Early this morning, two technicians were distributing the creatures daily ration of raw meat. After delivering the live cow to the cell, it proceeded to gorge on the poor animal as per usual, yet while, until now, it seemed to be very content on just one livestock, it sensed my colleagues were in attendance and before anyone could do something to stop it, it set upon them.

Charlie was the first to die. His deathly screams will haunt me for the rest of my life. The creature picked him up like a doll and attacked so viciously it was reminiscent of the fate of an antelope in a lion's den.

And then there was Betty. She did well to raise the alarm.

What she saw must have been worse than any nightmare the most fervent imagination could dream up.

While it was feasting on her colleague she was able to tear herself away from the horror and call for help, but as she made for the safety gates, she realized that their key was on Charlie's person, and there was too little of Charlie left at this point to be of any help in her escape.

Until now we hadn't any reason to think that the creature would harm us.

Well, I have, truth be told, but yet it has never seemed to harm us, no matter how often we seem to harm it.

It was simply a precaution to keep the doors locked. But mistakes happen and that's when lessons are learned.

It's just a terrible, terrible tragedy and a shame that we had to learn that lesson in such a harsh way.

Rob retched. He dare not read on and yet he felt compelled to. It was clear to him now that the treatment the monster had endured in the name of progress had driven it over the edge. But now it was awake, after what must have been nearly 70 years of sleep, waiting for the opportunity to kill again.

He continued:

When the creature had finished draining the life force out of Charlie, it made for Betty. At this point I and several others entered the room. If it hadn't been for Betty's cries we would have abandoned all sense and awareness and done nothing else but run for our own lives.

Some of the technicians made for the cattle prods. I stayed well back out of the action and allowed those more skilled to tackle the beast. Hurriedly, I called for medical assistance.

Other members of our team also held their nerve and dragged Betty out of the cage as the sound of her screams of agony and the electrical charges of the cattle prods flooded the air.

I could barely bring myself to look upon her mutilated frame. The stench was indescribable. I have not smelt death like it since Flanders. The poor girl was still alive, scrambling for something, anything to cling on to. I surveyed her injuries. Both legs were gone, one just below the left knee and the other completely. Her arms were still there, but one dangled on a thin line of torn flesh. The crimson, copper smell of blood caused me to vomit discreetly in the corner. The cries of Betty were piercing, as were the hellish shrieks of the creature.

Whitehall will have to hear about this. It could mean the end of the whole project. The animal will have to be put down.

I cannot see any justification that it should be allowed to live any longer. The horrible, genetic experiment has, in my mind, been a total and utter failure. Instead of using what limited resources we have at hand to build what I proposed – an extract that could make our men on the front line faster and more agile than our enemies – we have created a demon on Earth. There's no knowing what it would do if it were let loose.

We were finally able to contain it, but in doing so, the Batallion General was informed right away. He is returning to the complex in two days but for me, the damage has already been done.

What were to happen if we could contain the monster no longer? My wife and children live not five miles from our test location. If we do not destroy it now then it could break free of the complex altogether and run amok. What will we, and I, be remembered for then?

What we have done, here, in these walls, is something which no living man should ever have the power to do.

We have played God over creation, and we have failed.

If we do not act soon, mark my words, it will be the end of us all.

I shall prey for Betty tonight. I checked with our medical team here at this base. They are not sure that they can save the arm. Mutilated beyond almost all recognition, I am not sure I can stomach a visit, even though she is under heavy sedation. There are fears tonight that she could develop sepsis or gangrene, and I know that if I were in her shoes I would probably encourage the staff to end her life now. It's no way for a human to keep on living.

As for Charlie, there was nothing left.

The creature had completely torn him to pieces, feasted upon his person and extinguished any sign of life.

It is truly a monster. And I must see that it be put to an end.

'Jesus Christ!' Rob swore.

He could barely keep the notepad steady as he shook in fear.

A shock of dread poured through every fibre of his being.

This creature was capable of tearing humans' limb from limb.

The torture implements had been designed to keep it in order but it had in fact made it stronger.

It fed off pain.

He resisted temptation to read anymore for fear of a severe fit of vomiting at the terrifying details the doctor had described.

He must get out and tell the police.

But what would they do? You'd need a whole army to put an end to the savage beast.

Maybe if he found a way out, he would somehow put it to sleep again? Maybe it was only when people were close by that it woke up?

'I mean, if it can stay alive all that time when the hangar was desolate, with so much traffic driving past over the last seventy-odd years, surely it will just hibernate again?' he thought out loud.

Rob rolled up and pocketed the notes then got up from his chair. He searched for signal again.

He cried in anguish as the bars were still showing nothing.

'Maybe if I could get to the control tower?' he theorised.

'Yeah, great idea Sherlock! Trap yourself in a tower when a raging monster is trying to kill you, and how many horror films have you seen in your life, you moron!?'

The trouble was, it did seem like a good idea. He had been chased deep into the bowels of the complex and there had been no doors, barely windows even, that would lead him to salvation. Hell, he hadn't even come across one solitary fire exit.

Whatever the hangar had been designed to do it was definitely more like a prison than an air base.

Rob had a choice to make. Continue searching for a way out or head for the tower? In the end, he decided to do both. The higher up he got, the more chance of him finding signal.
And the closer to the tower, maybe the greater the chance of an escape.

It stirred. The gash to its head had almost healed. It knew it would do that.

Its metabolism had been one of its greatest allies when it was relentlessly attacked way back when.

The power from the cattle prods had made it stronger, less impervious to danger. It opened its eyes, blinking as a slight headache began to melt away.

The human had been very fortunate. Luck was truly on its side so far. The creature had managed to strike its cranial soft spot on the wall.

There's no way it would have been stunned if it had hit its intended target but it was rusty after such a long time dormant.

Now that the dust had been shaken from its aged bones, the creature began to pull itself to full size.

It engulfed the little office it had awoken in.

Although slim and agile, its full height made it almost burst through the ceiling.

How fortunate it was that it could stand on two or all four of its legs.

It sniffed the air.

The human was gone.

It growled an ungodly cry, one of anger and embarrassment.

In its prime, it would never have been so foolish.

It did not know how long it had been since it fed, but it had been a very, very long time.

It took a look around as its black, demonic eyes darted from left to right, unblinking.

It remembered this room.

This was one of the first places it had fled to after the break out.

It knew, because its claw marks adorned the walls and floor, as did the streaks of blood.

It had brought death and devastation to its prison.

And yet it could not quite remember why it was unable to leave?

If there were humans inside the complex, so very long ago, then surely there were humans outside?

But why hadn't it found the strength to leave?

The creature put that thought to one side, for now, and started to make after its prey yet again.

Slow and steady, it made its way down the corridor, following the scent that Rob was unintentionally laying.

Perhaps, the creature thought to itself as its multiple sets of razor sharp teeth salivated once more, one more meal would give it the strength to break free from its captivity once and for all…

III

Claire would be wondering where he was. He knew it. Deep down, no matter how cross she got with his bone-idled tendencies, how often he infuriated her with his lack of attention, at least she always cared.

Maybe that's why I'm such a shit, he pondered as he wheeled up the winding steps. The lift was out of service, of course it was! Since he had managed to jam the door behind him, he felt a little safer than before. Okay, yes, he reminded himself, he had seen the creature turn a whole door frame into splinter wood, but as he gained height, his predicament felt less hopeless.

Claire dominated his thoughts.

He continued to glance nervously at his phone, willing its battery life to last and for the signal bar to pop back into existence.

Maybe that was the problem with him? He knew he could always depend on her. Yet she could never depend on him.

As he wound up the staircase, he began to list the terrible things he had done.

He had forgotten to turn up to her Dad's 60th birthday. There she was, slaving away with the meal preparation, dressing the house up, ready for her extended family and his long-term friends, all by herself.

She called him, lots of times, and since she had moved down to Cambridge to be with him, away from her own family and friends, she didn't feel like she knew that many people to call upon to help her out.

He winced at the memory. She must have called at least 30 times.

And what did he do?

He slept in. A heavy night out at a friend's house in London had put pay to any chances of him getting to their home in time for the party to begin.

He had promised he would help out. He promised he would be home in time to set up. He promised she would not have to do it all alone. Moving away had been difficult enough for her. She had made a big sacrifice for him and although she didn't really want to stop him from going, he knew deep down she didn't want him to go in case he couldn't keep his promise.

And of course, like the selfish bastard he was, he didn't keep it.

Rob had set an alarm, just to be sure. He would have enough time to sober up on the tube and then finally on the overground train from Liverpool Street, he could sleep off the dregs of a night of partying.

But he had turned his phone on silent and slept through right until mid afternoon.

By then, it was too late for redemption. Even as he made his way on the bus, he realised he was wearing one of his friend's shoes and one of his own. He had wondered why it was pinching around his toes.

He looked down at his shirt. There was a beer stain clinging to the front like a bad memory.

And when he finally arrived, it was the silence from Claire that really burrowed into his heart.

He had fucked up. Again.

This hadn't been the first time. Oh no.

What about the girl she caught him in bed with when they first started dating?

Even though they were not yet official, of course she was going to take that kind of revelation badly. Who wouldn't?

If it had been him walking in on her, her legs wrapped around the heaving hips of a lover hitherto unknown to himself, he probably would have taken a couple of months to talk to her again too.

Or possibly never.

Why had she put up with him?

He was a twat. He knew it.

But that was the old him, he had tried so hard recently to put that life and his old ways behind him.

He quit drinking. Okay, well, maybe not quit, but he wasn't putting away as much as he had been in the past.

He had quit smoking; although he would have done anything for a cigarette in his current predicament.

He had sharpened up his act. He was making sure he was getting to work on time every day, going to sleep earlier so he didn't look like a zombie as he went about his administrative duties.

Hell, he had even taken Claire out on more dates and yet she still flew off the handle with him, on tonight of all nights, and it hadn't really been his fault.

Rob breathed hard as he neared the top of the tower.

He deserved none of this and yet at the same time he deserved every bit of bad karma that came his way.

He was paying for his sins of the past.

And tonight, he could end up losing everything.

If only he could get signal, he could call her, tell her what's happened.

She'd probably have a go at him at some point for crashing the car. That was a given. It was Claire's after all.

But how was he going to explain to her that a monster from the stuff of nightmares had trapped him in an old abandoned secret aircraft complex that they had driven past dozens of times and yet never seen?

That he possibly had uncovered a government plot to build super creatures to fight against the Nazi's in World War Two?

Of course she wouldn't believe him!

At that moment, a thought popped into Rob's head.

He had a camera phone.

Of course! He could take pictures of the documents he had found, that'd be proof enough surely!

Better still, why not keep them in his pocket. They could be verified by the authorities!

Rob laughed to himself. She would believe him. She'd have to. This time he had an excuse that couldn't be disproved!

Even better still…he could take a picture of the creature itself.

Rob's eyes widened. Could he face it again?

He seemed safe now. Maybe it had lost his scent?

No, it was too risky.

The creature would tear him apart. What if it broke free from its prison? What if it followed him to freedom? Who could stop it then?

He sighed as he reached the top of the tower and pushed against the heavy metal door that opened onto the control room.

He blinked as his eyes adjusted.

There was less darkness up here compared to the other parts of the complex. Furthermore, the occasional flashes of lightning lit up the room, illuminating its retro glory. Noticing a piece of metal on a nearby desk, Rob smiled as he discovered an open box of ancient cigarettes and a shiny lighter. Shaking it, he sighed gratefully. It felt full of fluid. But would it work?

Flicking the lid back, it sparked into life. Rob's eyes glowed with hope.

This little lighter would save precious battery juice on his phone.

Gratefully, he slid a cigarette out of the back, popped it in his mouth and lit it. The rush of nicotine reinvigorated him. Just one, Claire would never know. He decided to save the lighter and pocketed it, before turning back to the cigarettes and pocketing them also.

It was substantially cleaner up here than in the office rooms Rob had been pursued into.

It looked like something from a film. A vast mountain of switches, lights and machinery that at one time must have been a hive of life. But now, nothing.

There was no life up here. None at all. No evidence that the creature had made its way up here.

The control room was hexagonal in shape, with glass windows surrounding all six sides, giving

Rob an impressive view as he gazed longingly through the dirty glass. Not far away, there lay what was left of his car. It was burning a bright orange, but there were no cars driving past to stop and raise the alarm for the accident.

Not one.

He could make out in the not-so-far distance towns and villages, faraway lights of life blinking through the shower of rain that continued to cascade out of the sky. Freedom was so close.

If he had been feeling extremely brave, he could have smashed one of the windows and used the old fire hose kept neatly against the wall to climb his way down away from this hellish nightmare.

But even if he was brave enough, even if he could have summoned up a superhuman fearlessness and even if he wasn't hindered by a slight fear of heights, the rain was coming down so hard that it would make it hard for anyone to keep their grip long enough to make it to the ground safely.

Still, it was a solution he might have to resort to using.

Taking another drag, he looked around for any further clues to the creature's origins but, alas, nothing. Maybe this control room was just for the nearby airfield?

There certainly wasn't anything to stop the monster from coming up here. Not with its superior strength.

Rob pondered whether there was anything in the notes he had swiped that may answer his question. Rob grabbed at a nearby lighter that sat on one of the control panels. Another one! Thank god that people back in the old days were so unhealthy, he thought.

He checked to see if it still sparked and luckily, a tiny flame emitted from within its metallic housing.

However, this one soon went out, drained of life, so he threw it down on the floor and immediately stiffened. What a stupid thing to do. He waited for a few moments, to see if the creature had heard him, his hideaway revealed.

Not a sound.

Rob exhaled hard. Reaching into his pocket, he sparked the first lighter and made for somewhere to sit down.

He sat on one of the complex banks of instruments and, manoeuvring himself against the window pane, he leant back and scurried through the paper looking for clues. Using his mobile phone now, with the battery almost dead, would be suicide.

Eventually, he came to something that looked of interest:

There's nothing we can do. It's ruined. It's all ruined.

Our hopes of controlling the beast have come to nothing. Upon learning that it was drawing power from our restraining rods, we have managed to seal off the east wing of the complex.

Management have all but conceded that this test has been a failure. We have not found a way to control the creature and sadly, there have been more casualties.

As a result of this, I can conclude that the creature leeches off the life force of everything.

It can consume electrical current in a way no-one has ever seen.

I have seen it drink blood like some kind of hellish vampire. It devours flesh and bone like they were kindling to fire.

I have lost colleagues to its might.

I am not worried about what I do next with my professional life. No. My concern turns to how we kill it. Do we drown it? Do we try to destroy it with a missile strike? Both these things have been written off by the higher ups as non negotiable acts that we must never carry out.

I too am of their thinking, for once, as if we bomb the base and the monster survives, it would be let loose, free to kill.

I know not of any swimming pools or lakes big enough so that we can transport it to dunk it like a witch of old, so what other choice do we have?

We must abandon the area.

If there is one glimmer of hope and happiness in recent times it is this.

The war effort is turning in our favour.

Hitler's men are starting to retreat. With the combined efforts of our boys and the Yanks, large areas of France have been liberated. We are pinning them back in their cages and who knows, by this time next year maybe the world will be saved and the Nazis gone.

I hope to Christ it happens.

But what of the demon in our midst?

According to our tests, the longer it goes without feeding, the weaker it gets. So to this conclusion, we can only hope that we can keep it caged and trapped within these walls.

We, its creators, torturers and possibly executioners, have conceded much of the area. The creature has torn through much of the building already but it stays away from the control tower. My colleagues have theorized this may be down to the creature needing to stay at ground level – maybe it suffers from vertigo?

There is no reason or rhyme as to why this might be the case but for all it's killing and rampaging, we have yet to see it go near that part of the base.

Some of us have resorted to camping out in the tower for safety. Those of us who are still here. The mauling of Betty was too much for many of my team and I understand why. Those who have remained are mainly military but in all reality I do not know why.

On many of its bloodthirsty rampages, they have opened fire with no regard for ammunition or safety of those near it.

And did they stop it? No. Bullets cannot kill it.

The creature is truly indestructible.

We have created a monster…and now we must starve it to death.

I am not sure of how long it will take the beast to perish. It could be weeks, it could be months. But I hope that this, the last resort, will work.

For humanity's sake.

This is my last log on the creature before I leave the complex. I must retrieve what I can from my office before I go. I understand how dangerous this will be, but there is vital information detailing the creation of the demon, that I must destroy. If anyone was to find what I have documented and replicate what we have done, if the Nazis do miraculously fight back and this war rages for years upon years until they do vanquish this green and pleasant land, then I must make sure that they do not do what we have done here.

I am part to blame. I have contributed towards giving this monster life. I must now contribute towards its extinction by destroying all that I have accomplished here.

There has been far too much bloodshed in recent times.

My creation has killed.

I pray to God that one day he will have mercy on my soul.

If I fail in my task…my God have mercy on us all.

The writing stopped.

Rob sighed. The body in the office, that was who wrote these notes. He had them with him. The secret to how the creature came about.

The scientist never had a chance to destroy his secret.

The scientist who never made it home to his family. There had been no sign of any other corpses, unless, perhaps he couldn't live with what he had created? Maybe he was the last one out? Whatever the conclusion, Rob understood the tremendous guilt he must have felt and the responsibility must have been overwhelming.

Somehow this creature had survived in hibernation for decades, but Rob's presence in the abandoned base had awoken it, possibly just at the point of its death.

For now, his course was clear. He would stay up in the tower until morning, at which time he would sneak downstairs, with the scientist's notes in hand, past the monster and off to freedom. If he had to walk to the nearest village he would bloody well do it.

But would he tell the police? If this is a government cover-up, then maybe it would be best if he kept it quiet. Maybe if he only told Claire, showed her the notes, then she'd believe him and they could forget about this hellish night.

Something flickered from the corner of Rob's eye. He turned to face the window. One of the villages had seemingly just blipped out of existence.

He turned his head again as another village appeared to blink into darkness.

'Oh shit!' he uttered.

All around him the light began to flick off.

'Power cut, surely?' he said.

He checked his phone again. No bars and the battery life had fallen to 3%.

'Shit, shit, shit, shit!'

He rummaged around the room looking for something to charge his phone with. Then he slapped his forehead and remembered how long the place had been abandoned. There was no chance that anyone had a mobile phone way back in the 1940s.

As the control room fell into black, with nothing but lightning to illuminate Rob's surroundings, he scrambled for his lighter.

All of a sudden, Rob heard the unearthly roar of the beast. It sounded quite far away, but it had found him.

Rob shuddered.

He was trapped.

IV

Rob peeked his head around the control room door. The creature screeched again, its cry curdling his blood. It sounded like it had stopped outside the door at the bottom of the stairs.

There it was, taunting him, mocking his inability for courage, to take it on or to escape from it.

He wiped the sweat from his brow with the back of his sleeve and raced to the notes on the control panel.

Feverishly, he rummaged for the lighter in his pocket, struck it into life and flicked quickly through the papers.

There had to be something in there, some clue as to how he could defeat the beast.

But there wasn't. Deep down, he knew there wasn't.

The creature roared its death cry once again, sending icy fear through Rob's nerves, sending him into frenzy.

Slowly, the terrible horror of his continued predicament overcame him like a black cloud.

If he was lucky enough to leave, escape this nightmare, then the monster could follow him.

It would follow him.

He would lead it to the rest of mankind.

To freedom.

Rob squeezed his eyes shut tight. He held them closed long enough for them to produce tears.

The realisation that he may never leave the base alive had begun to dawn on him.

Sniffing, he turned over a page of notes and read back a paragraph of the scientist's last entry.

There was nothing in the notes that suggested it would not be impervious to fire.

The creature howled again, this time louder, perhaps closer than before. Maybe it wasn't put off by the control tower after all?

It waited for him.

It was tired, its patience waning.

Tentatively, it rested a claw on the door and pushed it open.

It stepped through.

Then it saw the stairs. There was nothing holding it back now.

He shivered.

Not from his sopping clothes, but from the fear as he heard the beast making its way up the creaky stairs.

'Please God, please, I beg you.'

Although he didn't believe in anything and held religion in contempt, Rob's last resort wasn't going to get him anywhere.

A plea to a God he didn't believe existed was a desperate straw to clutch, and why would anyone want to save him?

The lazy, selfish cheat who always put himself first. Unredeemable.

He forced himself up off the floor and began to search the cupboards for something, anything he could use to fend off the creature, no matter how futile.

Tears pouring down his face, his efforts were fruitless.

Until…

'What the?'

Rob blinked.

Were his eyes playing trick on him?

Inside the last open cupboard, closest to the door, were jars of what looked, and smelt, like paraffin.

The smell was intoxicating, having been kept

away behind closed doors for decades.

Rob grinned like a maniac.

He could do it.

He could kill the creature.

He could redeem himself.

The escape was back on and in the process he wouldn't just be saving himself.

He would be saving the world.

He began to bring the jars out of the cupboard and splash them around the control tower, taking care not to get any on himself.

If he could hide, lure the creature inside, he could trap the monster and make good his escape by sliding down the banister to liberation.

The monster sounded excruciatingly close now as he heard it thunder up the stairs.

Rob took his shirt off and fed it into the near empty jar, ran to the nook just behind the door and crouched down, lighter at the ready.

He had to time it just right, otherwise he would be burnt to a crisp along with the beast.

Quietly, he took several deep breaths, as if summoning up the courage to do what he was about to.

The rumbling of what sounded like hooves stopped.

Rob's hand shook as he primed the lighter.

The monster sniffed and screeched outside the door.

It hissed an inhuman sigh before bellowing a noise so terrible a trickle of liquid began to emanate from Rob's trouser leg.

To his horror, the monster tore the doors to shreds and burst into the control tower, a demon in the dark.

Rob bit his lip hard to halt a scream that threatened to burst in the air.

The creature bounded into the room and swung itself around searching for the scent of its prey.

But all it could smell was the sickly smell of paraffin.

It roared.

Without a moment to lose, Rob lit his shirt and hurled the paraffin jar at the monster. It exploded on impact in a shower of brilliant orange, sending it reeling into the control panels, shattering glass and metal as it fell.

A shriek of horrible, horrible pain burst from the fireball that now engulfed the monster and as it swung itself from side to side to put the flames that engulfed it out, it created more fire.

Rob tore himself away from the brilliant explosions of light that illuminated the room and hurled his frame through the decimated doors as the heat began to fry his skin.

The monster continued to writhe in agony, it's terrible shrieks surely audible for miles around.

Rob picked himself up as the flames began to lick the stairwell and mounted the stair rail before throwing himself down. He kicked his feet off the floor and let gravity dictate his journey as he looked back. Squinting through the flames, for a split second, he witnessed the creature destroying its surroundings, flailing in vain to extinguish the fireball. The crashing and sound of the flames echoed as Rob descended towards the ground floor.

His mind searched for something cool to say, like the kind of thing action film stars would give as a one-liner, but nothing came to him.

The stairwell must have been ten stories tall and he struggled to keep his body on the railing as it continued to spiral down, down into the gloomy darkness.

Rob cried out as he used his hands as brakes but he wasn't slowing down. If anything, he was picking up speed.

The friction on his palms started to open his skin. Although the pain was excruciating he had to keep going, had to get to the bottom but it was becoming unbearable.

Rob kicked his feet out from underneath him and tried to use his heels as a wedge to catch on the stairs and decrease his speed even more.

It was a costly mistake.

With no more than two floors to go, his foot caught on one of the iron bars that helped keep the railings upright and his body was catapulted forward.

His helpless form slammed hard down the stairs and into the wall at the base of the shaft.

The next thing he remembered, as he blinked back unconsciousness, was a distant glimmer of light at the very top of the stairwell and that unearthly cry of terror.

'Jesus! Come on!' he spat as he clambered to his feet.

He crumpled to the floor again and cradled his ribs. Breathing heavily, he wheezed as he felt them, two of which felt jagged and protruded against his skin in an unnatural manner.

He screamed, they were both screaming at opposite ends of the stairwell, both in terrible agony.

His head and arm had also begun to throb and his left ankle felt like it was ballooning too.

The cry came from way down below.

The creature leered forward out of the control room. Its skin was melting, molten flesh hanging from its tortured body.

And still it burnt.

The monster began to cry to itself. A horrific, unspeakable agony tormented it.

The pain was indescribable. It limped to the stair rail as the control room fire began to spread outside of its confinement.

It wouldn't go on.

It couldn't go on. Not like this. Not with the heat of the flames shredding its nervous system, tormenting its muscles, firing a void of eternal agony in every conceivable part of its body.

It would die. It knew that this was now its fate.

But the cry from far below had stirred one last ounce of strength and determination within its mutilated remains.

Its attacker had to pay.

Whimpering softly, Rob used the wall to steady his broken frame as he slowly got to his feet. He gazed upwards, trying to block the pain out but started to panic when he saw the creature's still-alight silhouette start to gain on him.

'Impossible. How?' he spat.

How was it still alive? It can't be impervious to fire too, could it? Surely it must have been injured!?

Rob didn't wait around to answer his own questions. He limped through the door and back out onto the base.

As he soldiered on, he took the engagement ring out of his pocket and clung onto it tightly.

He willed Claire to be with him, to give him strength.

His mind began to will her into existence. He began to hear her soft, soothing voice.

'Come on, babe, you can make it! Please come back to me, please! I forgive you. I'll forget everything bad you have done as long as you come back to me. I don't know what I would do without you. You're a mess, but you're my mess. I love you…do it for me.'

If his phone had worked, if he had remembered to charge it at work, if it had at least one bar of signal, after he had explained his predicament, after she'd have heard the blood curdling screams from the creature, she would have believed him, he had absolute faith in that.

And she'd have forgiven him for all of his past flaws just to return home safe and sound.

They could always rebuild, couldn't they? Become stronger and more loving as a couple?

When he got down on one knee, she'd have said yes, wouldn't she?

The creature tore downstairs, hurling its body at the wall in a bid to quench the flames as it spiraled deeper and deeper towards the base and closer to the human coward that was trying to escape its deathly clutches.

As its injured form continued on and on, gaining pace, running through the barrier of anguish its injuries had created, it started to feel stronger.

It knew it was as good as dead, but the flame of life would not go out before it had wreaked revenge.

'Come on, Rob, you can do this, you can do this. You're almost there. Do it for her, you big loser!'

The corridors began to wind around familiar nightmares that he had lived very recently. He had made it past the scientist's office and moved through the waiting room-like area where he had read the notes.

Before long, he was almost back in the hangar where this nightmare had started.

The escape route was almost in sight.

But so was the creature.

Rob heard it first. It sounded like a stampede was heading his way.

As he made it into the hangar, he threw himself to the adjacent wall. He couldn't outrun it.

Not anymore.

He was mere metres away from the hole under the door that had brought him inside the base.

But there it was. The creature, despite the isolated flames that seemed to burn on different parts of its body, still stood in the darkness from which it seemed to be born.

His face dropped. So near. So close.

'Listen, listen to me,' he gibbered. 'Please, before you do anything to me, I know what you are, I know what you were meant to be. I won't tell anyone, do you here?

I-I-I, my lips are sealed, do you understand me?

I didn't mean you any harm, I'm sorry for what I have done, but I'll make a deal with you.

Let me go, I won't tell anyone that you are here, just please,' Rob fell to his knees and clasped his hands together. His mobile phone and engagement ring met in the middle.

'I'm not like the others, I know what they did to you was wrong, so wrong, but that was a long time ago. Please, I j-just want to go home. I've got a girl waiting. Well, I h-hope she's still waiting for-'

It wasn't supposed to end this way.

It leered closer, gazing with filthy black eyes through the gloomy darkness, the finality of death lusting deep within its unholy stare.

An inner turmoil boiled within him, a resistance to not look the creature dead in the eyes and a yearning to see it in all its terrifying glory. He chose the second and instantly wished he hadn't. Now he was transfixed, there was no turning away. He had to look, had to make sure that in this, what was sure to be his final moment, he was brave until the last.

For his Mother and Father, for all who had ever cared for him.

For her…

The creature had heard enough.

With a mighty swing of its arm, it wiped Rob clean off the floor and across the hangar. He hurtled through the air before landing painfully on the cold floor.

Fighting blackout, he was so close to the exit point. He scrambled with all his might and began to pull himself back through the hole into the cold, wet, stormy night.

But all the creature was doing was giving him hope. The cruelty of its delay was the last injustice Rob ever felt.

As the monster grabbed him by his broken ankle and hauled his frame, kicking and screaming like a toddler, back inside hell, it gazed at its final victim.

The last thing Rob ever saw would haunt him in whatever lay past the inevitability of death.

It was its eyes, those black harrowing eyes.

They were the eyes of the devil himself.

Rob's screams could be heard from outside the hangar. But no one was on the road side to hear him.

As the fire continued to rage in the control tower, a sight that had alerted someone in a nearby village to call the fire brigade, the beast devoured its first victim in a long, long time, bit by bit.

Its needle like teeth ripped at Rob's flesh. He had screamed for a while until the beast had reached his vital organs and finally put him out of his misery.

Before long, the rage and anger that had consumed the beast like the fire that had wounded it, started to waver. Now its prey was dead, there seemed little point in continuing its slaughter.

As blood poured from its open mouth, droplets of crimson dripping from its teeth, the creature roared its last.

Its final attack was over.

The wounds were all too much to bear now.

With one final roar, the creature slumped to the ground next to what was left of Rob and breathed its last.

All was silent in the hangar now. Nothing moved, no one breathed, nothing lived. The air was still as the smell of death hung in the atmosphere.

As the fire raged and the rain outside continued to cascade down, the lightening outside illuminated the hangar, exposing a sight so horrific it was a blessing there was no one to see it.

In the terrible mess that used to be Rob, his blood stained arms lay lifeless, reaching towards the hole he had climbed through into the unknowing nightmare, his finger tips wet from the rain outside.

Inside his still, outstretched palm, the phone lay motionless.

Nearly as dead as its owner, a signal bar suddenly flickered into life and as if it were meant to be, a phone call from Claire appeared on screen before the phone too gave into the cold embrace of death.

Acknowledgements

With thanks to Nicola Currie and Tom Savill-Owen for subjecting themselves to the first draft and helping me pull the story together.

As always my lovely wife Sophie, whose opinions and words of encouragement are always more appreciated than I can ever express.

To everyone who has ever bought or read one of my books. I cannot tell you how much it means when people say they have enjoyed my work. There is plenty more to come!

The Lurking is my first foray into horror and it was a nice change of pace, focus and an opportunity to work and challenge myself with a different genre.

And finally to the disused airfield in Little Walden, Essex and the ghost story my Father told me about that old, abandoned place. It fuelled my imagination as a boy and was the basis for this story.

Also Available:

Captain Random and the Eater of Souls

ISBN: 978-1999865931

Following their explosive battle with the Sandman, and struggling to come to terms with life out in space, the crew of the Venus II decide to throw themselves into a spot of retail therapy on the friendly planet of Genocia.

But almost as soon as they arrive, they realise that this new world is not all that it seems. Outside the splendour and vast wealth of the Grand Chamber lies a neglected wasteland where terror lurks within the poisonous gloom whilst deep within the bowels of the planet lies a terrible secret.

At the very heart of it all is the ruthless leader Consula, whose designs for supremacy mean ultimate devastation to all of those who oppose her. But the greed and corruption of the government is nothing compared to what lurks in the shadows for Random and his friends. Separated and fighting for their lives, Random, Anji, Jake and Skateboard must work quickly to save the lives of the prisoners stuck in the mines deep below the surface, where death is very close by...

What is the Soul Destroyer? What part does it play in Consula's diabolical plan? Will Anji ever see her friends again? One thing is for sure. The Eater of Souls is hungry...

Captain Random vs the Sandman

ISBN: 978-1999865924

Rodas. The scorned planet of Ursa-17. Ravaged by centuries of war between two factions, the villainous Sapphire Regime and the ruthless Crimson Empire. The reason behind the conflict of red and blue? The people of Rodas were unable to make the colour purple.
Until one day, when two rebels, one from either side, combine to create the ultimate warrior. A being who could put an end to the battle of ages and bring peace to the volatile planet of Rodas once and for all.

There is one tiny drawback. The warrior is a boy.

***** Fantastic book, enjoyed every part of it!
Highly recommend it for Dr Who/Red Dwarf/Rick and Morty fans.

***** Hayden Gribble's writing is witty and clever with an essence of Douglas Adams in there too. Would thoroughly recommend for anyone with an adventurous spirit.

***** I really enjoyed it. I can well imagine Kids getting swept along with the interstellar, action packed adventure and chuckling along with all the funny scenarios and characters and wanting to know just what happens .

Available from all good book shops.

Child Out of Time: Growing Up With Doctor Who in the Wilderness Years

ISBN: 978-1999865900

For 26 years, DOCTOR WHO was a British institution, capturing the imaginations of generations of children. But then, in 1989, it was cancelled. The Doctor and his on-screen adventures were no more. There was no longer a hero, a champion for the outcasts who struggled to fit in. It was as though he had walked into his TARDIS and set his controls for dematerialisation, never to return: a whole generation lost to the powers of Science Fiction's greatest creation. It was in this Doctor-less world that I grew up. This is the story of how one little boy would try to find the Doctor in any way, shape or form and the obstacles he faced in doing so. This is the story of growing up without Doctor Who in the Wilderness Years…and how I lived through it.

***** An engaging and enjoyable insight into a fan discovering Doctor Who during the wilderness years

***** A very passionate account of one fans discovery of the greatest science fiction of all time.

**** Perfect for fans of the Doctor in any of his or her forms.

Available from all good book shops.

The Man In The Corner

ISBN: 978-1500549862

A mysterious assassin wants out of his life as a cold and ruthless killer but must face one last assignment before he flicks the escape switch. As he closes in on the biggest criminal mind in the country, he is reminded of what he left behind and how getting closer to the light at the end of the tunnel might also reunite him with a person from his long and distant past. Who is the Big Chief? Why must he be brought down and will it be the end, not just for himself and his superior, but also to the only link to the life he has lost.

***** An exciting book! Whilst focusing on the dark story of an unnamed man, you find yourself sucked into a city of criminals. The chapters contain their own stories which really draw you in and make you want to read more. Great read! The only negative is that it was over too fast.

***** Brilliant read. Did not want to put the book down.

*** This book is a great little read about the path to redemption; not too long, in fact in some places I found myself wishing it might go on a little longer. It's got a sort of style all its own.

Available from all good book shops.

Hayden Gribble was born in Cambridge in June 1989. He has always loved writing and released his debut novel, The Man In The Corner, as an ebook in 2013 before it went paperback the following year.

The Lurking is Hayden's first horror short story and is his sixth book.

Away from writing, Hayden loves reading, walking, sports, music, film and TV.

He has also been a regular member of the Diddly Dum Podcast, a show about Doctor Who, since February 2015 and curates his own James Bond podcast, Podcasters Royale. Both can be found on iTunes.

He lives with his wife in Suffolk.

www.ingramcontent.com/pod-product-compliance
Lightning Source LLC
Chambersburg PA
CBHW071946190726

48293CB00004B/1376